Pob's Stories

Here is a delightful and varied collection of short stories and poems that television personality Pob, the puppet, has chosen, with a little help from his friend, Anne Wood.

Alan Garner, Marjorie Darke, Helen Cresswell, Berlie Doherty, William Mayne, Bernard Ashley and Naomi Lewis are just some of the authors. There are more. Look inside.

Pob's Stories

chosen by Anne Wood

illustrated by Jonathan Hills

Fontana Young Lions

First published in Great Britain by Fontana Young Lions 1986
8 Grafton Street, London W1X 3LA
Second impression July 1986

Fontana Young Lions is an imprint of
Fontana Paperbacks, part of
the Collins Publishing Group

This collection copyright © Ragdoll Productions (UK) Ltd 1986
Stories and poems copyright © by individual authors 1985
Illustrations copyright © Jonathan Hills 1986

Printed in Great Britain by
William Collins Sons & Co. Ltd, Glasgow

Contents

How nice to have you for a friend

NAOMI LEWIS

Since no one writes me a letter
A letter to me I'll send.
DEAR ME will be the beginning
and LOVE FROM ME the end.
And in the middle
      I'll say,
      I'll say,
HOW NICE TO HAVE YOU
FOR A FRIEND.

Emma's Monster

MARJORIE DARKE

"I don't want to go to bed," Emma said.

"It's half past six. You always go to bed then," said Dad.

"But I don't want to," Emma said, very loud.

Dad looked at her. "Why not?"

"Because there's a monster under my bed," Emma told him.

Dad put down his book. "I hoovered under your bed today. I didn't find any monster."

"He lives in a hole," Emma explained. "He only comes out at night."

Dad stood up. "Tell you what. How if I come upstairs with you and we look together? If the monster is there, I'll pick him up and take him away."

"He'll bite you." Emma showed all her teeth. "He growls 'URRG', and his teeth snap

8

snap, and he's got big red eyes."

Dad laughed. "I want to meet this splendid monster of yours. Come on!" and he went with Emma up to her room.

They knelt down and looked under the bed. There was a slipper, a ball and a feather. But no monster.

"He's hiding in that hole." Emma pointed behind her bed.

A mouse-sized hole!

"He must be a very little monster to squeeze in there," Dad said.

"Sometimes he's little. Sometimes he grows as big as a bus," Emma said.

Dad looked surprised. "A bus? In here? He wouldn't fit."

"A small bus." Emma took off her jumper.

Dad helped with shoelaces, and when she was in her pyjamas and had cleaned her teeth, tucked her up in bed. "When you see the monster, tell him to come down and watch telly with me."

"He doesn't like telly." Emma wriggled down under the bedclothes.

Dad kissed her. "Ask him and see. You never know!" and he went out leaving the door ajar.

Emma lay in bed. The moon came in and made silver stripes on her wall. A moth flew round and round and round. She was almost asleep when . . .

"URRRG!"

The monster's noise! Her eyelids flew open.

"URRRG, URRRRRRG!"

She was very surprised and just a bit scared. No pretending, this monster was real! She opened her mouth to shout for Dad.

"Snuffle snuffle chatter chatter rattle hiccup."

It didn't sound like a fierce monster. Emma shut her mouth and wriggled to the edge of her bed. Carefully she looked over and under.

Two big red, upside-down eyes stared back at her. A *very* small monster. Not fierce at all. He was shivering. His long arms shook. His wild, wild hair trembled. His big teeth chattered. His pointed ears quivered. His little round face looked crinkled with cold.

Cold and *scared*, Emma thought, feeling not scared at all. She got out of bed and picked up her jumper.

"Put this on and get warm."

The monster crept from under the bed and Emma helped him put on the jumper. The arms were rather short, but he didn't mind.

Then they played ball. And blowing the feather. The monster's long arms reached the other side of the room to catch the ball; to pick up the feather. He grew, not as big as a bus, but chair-sized—and shrank again. His big red eyes shone bright as torches, so they sat in bed and looked at a picture book until they were tired. Then they lay down and went to sleep together.

"Your monster didn't turn up after all," Dad said to Emma at breakfast next morning.

"Yes, he did," Emma said. "But he didn't want to come downstairs. I like telly but he doesn't. I *told* you."

The Teeth-Tidier

RACHEL ANDERSON

Arthur's Gran came to stay. She had the other
bed in Arthur's room. So Arthur moved his
toys out of the way to give Gran somewhere
to put her things. Arthur thought it would be
good having Gran to stay because she always
had time to read to him but after the first day,
Arthur said to his mum,

"How much longer has she got to stay
here?"

"Why?" said his mum. "Don't you like
your gran?"

"I don't like her teeth," said Arthur.

"What's wrong with them? Everybody has
to have teeth or they couldn't eat anything
except porridge."

"I don't mind the teeth in her face," said
Arthur. "It's the ones by the bed I don't like.
They look at me in the morning."

Arthur didn't say anything to his gran
about the teeth because he didn't want to upset her. Mostly, he liked her staying. She
wasn't in a hurry all the time. When she

walked him to playgroup, she let him stop on
the bridge and throw sticks in the river.

"They're false teeth," said Arthur's mum.
"That's why she has to take them out at
night."

"I know," said Arthur.

"And she puts them in the glass to clean
them."

Arthur knew that too.

"One day, when you're old, you might
have teeth like that."

"I shan't put them in a glass they can peek
out of," said Arthur.

13

He thought and thought about what he could do to stop the teeth frightening him. At playgroup, he had his idea.

After milktime, but before singing time, they had making things time. Ben was making a black mask for his big sister. Don was making a castle. Sam was making a snowman. Arthur knew exactly what he was going to make, and how to make it. He needed an empty cardboard box . . . the right size to fit over the top of a glass of water. The playgroup helper found the right one. Arthur painted it blue, then decorated it with pictures of interesting things. He asked the helper to help him write the words that say 'TO MY GRAN LOVE FROM ARTHUR' on top of the box.

"It's very nice," said the helper. "But whatever is it?"

"It's a teeth-tidier," said Arthur.

The helper put it to dry on the radiator.

When his gran came to collect Arthur from playgroup, he gave it to her.

"Ooh, thank you Arthur, ever so much," she said. "It's just right," and she gave him a big hug.

She understood exactly what it was for and

when she came to bed that night and put her teeth in the glass, she popped Arthur's decorated tidier tidily over the top.

When Arthur woke up in the morning, he couldn't see the teeth. Instead, he saw the decorated box, which didn't look at all frightening. In fact, it looked so good he thought he'd probably make his gran another one for her birthday.

Twelve Daisies

GERALDINE KAYE

Minty and Hopsy are travelling children. They live in a caravan hitched to a lorry. In summer, they stop in the country and pick strawberries with Pa and Ma but they never stop anywhere long. Minty and Hopsy like summer and strawberry-picking best. But one day Pa stopped on the empty space in Flower Street.

"When's it summer then?" Minty asked, looking out.

"Summer's when you can put your foot on twelve daisies," Pa said and he unhitched the caravan and drove off.

Minty took her doll, Araminta, outside. Pa made Araminta out of wood and Minty took her everywhere. Over the fence was a house and somebody singing. And when Minty looked through a gap she saw a girl Elizabeth, pushing a doll's pram on the other side. Minty wanted to say *Hello* but she was afraid of 'house people', so she just held Araminta above the fence instead.

"Hello," said Elizabeth and she climbed up and looked over.

"I'll play with your doll and you play with mine?" And she handed *her* doll over the fence and put Araminta into the pram and skipped off.

"Kushtie," whispered Minty, holding Elizabeth's doll. It was very beautiful with a lacy dress and eyes as blue as sky.

Suddenly Pa came back in the lorry.

"Can't stop here," Pa said and he hitched the caravan back to the lorry. "Can't stop anywhere long."

16

Minty was still holding the beautiful doll but all she wanted now was Araminta.

"Come on then," Hopsy said and he took Minty's hand and they ran to the house and rang the bell.

"Oh, Elizabeth's doll. Thank you for bringing her back," the lady said and she was just about to shut the door when Elizabeth came running down the stairs with Araminta.

Minty held Araminta tight against her chest and they ran back and climbed into the lorry with Ma and Pa and drove away.

When Minty woke in the morning there were daisies all round the caravan.

"Kushtie," said Minty and ran outside and put her foot on twelve daisies.

It was summer at last.

Two Trolls

HELEN CRESSWELL

Once upon a time in a deep dark hole in a deep dark wood there lived two trolls. Their names were Tig and Toggle.

They looked just like all the other trolls in the wood. They were just as ugly and hairy and their toes were just as dirty.(Trolls, you know, are downright mucky.) Oh, they *looked* like the other trolls, all right, but they weren't. As you know, trolls are not only mucky, they're bad as well. They get up to all kinds of tricks. But Tig and Toggle were *good*.

They didn't want to be. All the other trolls would yell,

"Ya boo! Goody goodies! You're goody goodies—we're the big bad trolls!"

And Tig and Toggle would creep into their hole and gnash their big yellow teeth with rage.

"Come on," said Tig to Toggle one day. "We're off to find something bad to do today. We'll be bad or bust!"

Off they set. As they went they stamped
their feet and shouted,

"We're Toggle and Tig and we're off to be bad, we're Toggle and Tig and we're off to be bad!"

The other trolls in the wood rolled their wicked black eyes and grinned their yellow teeth.

"They can't be bad if they *tried*!" they said one to another.

Tig and Toggle reached the edge of the deep dark wood. There in front of them was the house where old Mr Giles lived. It had a beautiful garden full of flowers and trees, and a wide green lawn. Mr Giles mowed his lawn twice every week. It was his pride and joy.

"Not a whisker of grass out of place!" he would say.

"Just look at that lovely smooth grass," said Tig.

"Not a whisker out of place," said Toggle.

"What if we dug a *hole* in it," said Tig.

"*Wouldn't* the old man be upset!" said Toggle.

"We'll dig it right in the middle," said Tig.

"We'll dig it *deep*," said Toggle.

They didn't need spades. Trolls use their horny fingers and toes to dig. Tig and Toggle dug like mad. Soil flew up in a shower.

"*Now* we're being bad, *now* we're being bad!" they muttered, as they dug. Soon the hole was very deep.

"Look out!" said Tig. "He's coming!"

The two trolls went scuttling back into the wood. There they hid in the bushes and stuffed their grubby fingers into their mouths to stop themselves laughing.

Mr Giles was carrying a small tree in one hand and a spade in the other. He stopped and stared.

"Good gracious me!" he said. "I can't believe it! Some kind person has dug a hole for my cherry tree!"

And he placed the roots of the tree in the hole, and began to fill it in with his spade.

"Digging holes is hard for an old man," he said. "What a lucky fellow I am!"

Tig and Toggle, hidden in the bushes, gnashed their teeth and stamped their feet. Behind them they could hear all the other trolls laughing and yelling,

"Goody goodies!"

Mr Giles stood back and looked at his beautiful new tree.

"I just wish I knew who to thank!" he said.

But we know, don't we?

Clean Clara

W. BLIGHTY RANDS
adapted by NAOMI LEWIS

What! not know our Clean Clara?
Why, the folk in hot Demerara
And the cold Esquimaux
They know, they know!

We all of us try to beware 'er.
"O Clean Clara! Oh, oh," we say.
"Let's hope she's not coming today!
Best keep out of her way!"

Last time she came, she gave us a shock.
She washed out the works of our best
    clock.
She scoured the springs of a secret lock.
She scrubbed the cat and she washed the
    mouse.
Nothing was left in peace in the house.

Tomorrow morning she means to fly
To do some cleaning up in the sky—
The stars and the clouds—oh, that can't
    be true!
But if you know Clara— she'll do it, too!

The Brush in the Hidey-Bush

BERLIE DOHERTY

Silvie has a hidey-bush at the bottom of her garden. It's so low that no one else can crawl under it. Nobody knows she's there when she's there. It's dark and quiet and as cool as mushrooms. Sometimes she goes into her hidey-bush to sing. And sometimes she goes in to play. And sometimes she goes in to eat her breakfast.

So there she was this morning, eating her cornflakes and singing a bit and smelling the lovely dark mushroomy smell when she stopped munching and said:

"Who's there?"

Someone was rustling round the leaves like a paper bag. The someone stopped, and after a bit Silvie had another mouthful of cornflakes, and then she said:

"Who's watching me?"

She looked round carefully. Sometimes robins hopped under the bush to have a word with her or a cat or a ladybird or two, but Silvie knew that it was none of these this time. What could it be? Then she saw it. It was a brush, round and small and spiky. And it was watching her.

"Oh," said Silvie. "It's only a brush." And she had another mouthful.

That was when the brush winked at her.

"What are you doing, brush, sitting in my hidey-bush, winking at me?" asked Silvie.

"I'm not a brush," the brush seemed to say, in a hurt, spiky sort of voice. Then Silvie saw four more brushes, rounder and smaller but just as spiky as the first, all rustling towards her through the leaves.

"I don't like brushes," thought Silvie. She put her bowl of cornflakes down, crawled out of her hidey-bush, and ran to find Grandma.

"My hidey-bush is full of brushes," she told her, even though she'd never told anyone about her hidey-bush before.

"Brushes?" said Grandma.

"Yes, brushes," said Silvie. "And they're all winking at me. And they're all after me. Come and see."

Just as they got to the hidey-bush, Grandma said, "Ssh! Listen!"

They crouched down on their hands and knees, and stayed so still that they hardly breathed. They listened. They could hear tiny little greedy tongues lapping. They lay on their tummies and pushed their heads carefully under the hidey-bush and they saw the five round spiky brushes with their faces in Silvie's bowl of cornflakes, lapping away like kittens. The biggest brush looked up. It had milk round its mouth. It winked at Silvie and Grandma and stuck its nose back into the bowl. Silvie and Grandma wriggled out, and Silvie pulled Grandma back onto her feet.

"They're not brushes, Silvie," said Grandma. "They're hedgehogs. And it's not you they're after. It's your breakfast. Aren't you a daft dumpling!"

Silvie knew she was. But she was a bit worried.

"Grandma," she said, as they had some more breakfast, "don't tell anyone about my hidey-bush, will you?"

And Grandma winked, just like a hedgehog, and promised that she wouldn't.

Spider in the Bath

DONALD BISSETT

Once upon a time there was a terrible battle. Snail charged. Grasshopper jumped. Kangaroo jumped. Flea jumped. Eli pushed with his head, and pulled the other way with his trunk. Tiger growled and snarled and bit— and who did Tiger bite?

He bit Crocodile. Bad, wicked Crocodile. What was bad Crocodile doing? He was trying to swallow the sun. The world grew darker and darker as the crocodile bit.

"What is to be done, beloved Snail?" said Caterpillar, who was pushing with his feet.

"Run Caterpillar. Run fast with all your legs and fetch Spider. Crocodiles are frightened of spiders," said Snail.

Caterpillar shot off like a bullet. Wheeeeeeeeee! He was the fastest caterpillar in the world.

Spider was crawling in the bath in mummy's house when Caterpillar arrived.

"Come quick, Spider!" he called. "Crocodile is swallowing the sun."

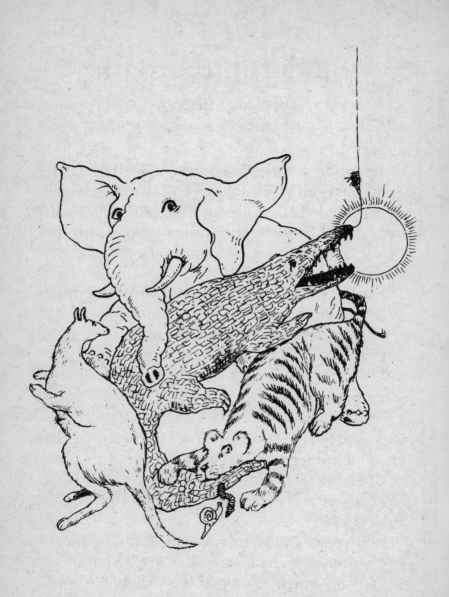

"I wondered why it was growing so dark," said Spider. "Help me out, please." (Spiders find it very difficult to get out of baths without help and they hate going down the plughole.)

As soon as he was out Spider ran fast—with his eight legs—and Caterpillar crawled fast with his hundred legs. They arrived at the river bank where all the animals were struggling.

Spider ran up Crocodile's back, then fixed some spider-thread to the end of Crocodile's nose. My, it was hot there, so close to the sun. But brave Spider let himself down on a thread right in front of Crocodile's eyes.

"Helllllllllp!!!!! HELP!!!!!!!!! A spider!!!!" shouted Crocodile, who let go of the sun and ran away as fast as he could.

"Hooray," called Snail.

"Hooray," called Flea.

"Hooray," called Grasshopper.

"Hooray," called some zebras, who had just arrived.

"Hooray," called Elephant and danced for joy.

"Hooray," called Kangaroo.

"Ugh!" said Tiger. "My mouth tastes of

Crocodile's tail. He dipped his mouth into the river, then went and fetched his toothbrush and cleaned his teeth. And then he had a lovely drink of water.

Crocodile, too, had gone to the river and hidden under the water. He looked out, with his eyes only. He couldn't see Spider. He breathed a sigh of relief.

"Don't you dare try to swallow the sun, again," said Tiger.

"I won't," said Crocodile. "My mouth is all sore and burnt. The sun is very hot."

"It is very very very very hot!" thought Spider, who had gone back to the bath. "Wouldn't it be terrible if Crocodile came along when the children were having their bath! I'll stay here to keep the crocodile away. And, at bath-time, I hope that mummy lifts me out very carefully onto a piece of paper."

Mummy did lift Spider out at bath-time that evening.

"Why was Spider in the bath?" asked the children.

"Why, to keep crocodiles away, of course!" said mummy.

Cry Baby!

BERNARD ASHLEY

"Stop your hollerin', child! Cryin' won't make me change me mind!"

Mrs Richards was pushing her trolley down the shop, turning her head away from the girl who was going on sobbing and screeching from her high seat.

"I want sweeties! I want Smartie-beans!" Pleasure was trying to stamp her feet—but you can't do that when they're dangling in the air.

"You get your sweeties at the weekend. Now, just you stop your noise or you'll get a smack to keep you goin'!"

But the child was working up a real temper.

"I want sweeties!" she yelled.

Mrs Richards stopped the trolley with a big jerk.

"What is your daddy goin' to say?" she shouted. "Wait till I tell him what a cry baby you been! Him thinkin' you're growin' up an' all! Oh, yes! 'She's my big girl,' he says. Well

I know different, don't I? Just cos you don' get what you want! He's headin' for a real big disappointment when I get you home!"

And that really shut Pleasure up, thinking of the look going to come on his face. She fell very quiet.

Outside the shop, they started walking for the bus, not in the mood for meeting a soul, but there was Mrs Powell from down their street, who'd seen them already and was waving.

"Hello, treasure—helping your mum with the shopping?"

The old lady gave her a smile. "Here, what have I got for a good girl?" With fumbly fingers, she unclicked her handbag and out came a great, big grown-up's sweet.

Now, Pleasure smiled too. "Thank you!" She took hold of the sweet and popped it in, quick. It was minty, not hard and not soft— took Pleasure's mouth a while to make up its mind what a nice taste it was—and so big it changed the shape of her face.

"Best taste going, that is!"

The old lady started walking off a different way, and Pleasure turned round to wave goodbye. But as she did, the too big sweet came out of her mouth, fell down and stuck on the pavement. Pleasure's eyes went big and filled up with tears. It wasn't fair! No sweeties for her in the shop—and now she'd dropped this special one out! And there was Mrs Powell still waving her hand.

"Nice, is it, love?" she called.

The whole street had come to a stop. Pleasure heard her mammy clear her throat, felt a shopping bag push at her leg to tell her to say something, quick.

With a bite of her lip, she looked up and stuck her tongue in her cheek, suddenly making the shape of the sweet.

"It's lovely," she said, doing a mouthful face.

The old lady went on her way, and Pleasure stared down at the dirty lump on the pavement.

"Never mind, pet!" her mammy said. "You know, I do believe you're my big girl after all! Won't your daddy sit up proud when I tell him how you just pleased that nice ol' lady?"

Teddy Lost

PHILIPPA PEARCE

Once upon a time there was a little girl called Sally. She lived with her mother and her teddy bear in a house with a green front door in a street called Elm Street. Sometimes, after breakfast, Sally's mother went shopping. Then she took Sally with her, and Sally took Teddy.

One morning, they set off shopping together. First, they went to the supermarket and bought some eggs. Then they went to the Post Office and bought some stamps. Then they went to a cafe, and Sally's mother had a cup of coffee and Sally had a strawberry ice-cream. Then they began to go home.

As they went home, Sally said to her mother, "Have you Teddy?"

Her mother said, "No. Haven't you?"

"No," said Sally, "Teddy's lost!"

So, of course, they turned back at once to find him.

First, they went to the supermarket and asked the lady who had sold them the eggs. "Have you seen a teddy bear? Did we leave a teddy bear here?"

The lady who had sold them the eggs said, "No, I've seen no teddy bear. You left no teddy bear here."

So then they went to the Post Office and asked the man who had sold them the stamps. "Have you seen a teddy bear? Did we leave a teddy bear here?"

The man who had sold them the stamps said, "No, I've seen no teddy bear. You left no teddy bear here."

So then they went to the cafe and asked the waitress who had brought them the coffee and the strawberry ice-cream. "Have you seen a teddy bear? Did we leave a teddy bear here?"

The waitress who had brought them the coffee and the strawberry ice-cream said,

"No, I've seen no teddy bear. You left no teddy bear here."

So they began to go sadly home. By now Sally was crying.

As they went, they met the milkman. The milkman knew Sally well, and he asked her: "Why are you crying?"

Sally said, "Because I've lost my teddy bear."

The milkman said, "Has your teddy bear got orange eyes?"

"Yes," said Sally. "Have you seen a teddy bear with orange eyes?"

The milkman said, "As I was passing your house with the green front door in Elm Street, I saw a teddy bear with orange eyes. He was lying on the pavement. So I picked him up and put him safely among my milk bottles. Go to the back of my milk van and seen if that teddy bear is yours."

So Sally went round to the back of the milk van and looked up. And there was Teddy sitting up among the milk bottles. He was holding out his arms to her. He was laughing his head off.

Sally stretched out her arms to Teddy and he jumped down into them. Then Sally took

Teddy in her arms and went round to the front of the van and thanked the milkman.

Then Sally and Teddy and Sally's mother all went home to lunch.

And that's the end of the story.

Swoosh!

NAOMI LEWIS

*This is about being in a swing. You can go higher
and higher and see all over the world. But you have
to look quickly because you are only up at the top
for a moment. You can't stay.*

Swing me, swing me high as the wall
To see what's over—no, I shan't fall.
*The swing will go as high as you say
But make the most of it while you may,
For you can't stay.*

Then swing me high, swing me high,
Over the high-rise, into the sky,
Higher up than a bird can fly,
Up to Jupiter! Up to Mars!
If it was night I could touch the stars!

*O.K., O.K.,
Whatever you say.
SWOOSH! SWOOSH! You are on your
    way!
But make the most of it while you may,
For you can't stay!*

Tom

CATHERINE STORR

When Tom was a very small boy, his grand-mothers and grandfathers and his aunts and uncles and cousins used to look at him and say,

"He has the family nose. It is just like Jack's and his grandpa's."

"He has hair like Aunt Em's."

"His eyes are exactly like mine," said one of his grandmas.

"And his chin is like my brother's, his great Uncle Harry," said a grandpa.

"He has ears just like his cousin Paul's," said an aunt.

"When he scowls he reminds me of old cousin Wilfred. I wonder if he will have a temper like that," said an uncle.

While Tom was quite small he didn't mind

this sort of talk. But when he grew older he didn't like it at all.

"Why do my eyes and my ears and my nose and my hair have to be like anyone else's? Why can't I just be me, Tom?" he asked.

He decided to show everyone that he was different from everyone else. He would do some extra-ordinary things. Tom stood on his head for five whole minutes and waved his legs in the air.

But his grandma said, "Look! That's just what his uncle Jack used to do."

SO THAT WAS NO GOOD.

Tom took off his clothes and painted himself green all over.

But his Aunt Em said, "I remember Tom's dad doing that. Only he painted himself blue, not green."

SO THAT WAS NO GOOD.

Tom jumped up and down forty-seven times and shouted, "Down with jelly babies!"

And his Uncle Peter said, "Funny! That's what I used to do when I was fed up with everyone around me."

SO THAT WAS NO GOOD.

At last Tom was so tired of his family that he decided to run away to find somewhere

where no one would say "Isn't Tom like . . . his grandpa . . . his aunt . . . his uncle . . . his cousin."

He walked out of his house and he walked and he walked and he walked. He walked a very long way, and he became very tired. When he stopped walking he was in a street he had never seen before. All the houses were strange and so were all the people. Suddenly Tom knew that he was very hungry as well as tired. He was missing his mum and his dad and he wished he had never run away so far from home. He tried to remember the way he had come so that he could go back. But he couldn't remember properly and soon he was more lost than ever.

Tom asked several people who passed him in the street, "Can you tell me how to get back to my house in Park Road?" But no one could tell him. He felt very sad and he did not know what to do next. But suddenly he saw a large red bus with the number SEVEN written on its front.

"Aha! The Number SEVEN bus goes near my street," Tom thought, and he began to walk in the direction in which the bus was going.

Presently, as he walked, Tom heard the
sound of a long, slow hoot.

"That is the hooter of one of the boats that
sails on the canal near where I live," Tom
thought, and he walked faster.

Then Tom smelled the smell of delicious new bread.

"I know that smell! It is the smell of the new bread that is baked every morning by Mr Georgias in his shop on the corner of my street," thought Tom, and he began to run, following the delicious smell. Almost at once he saw Mr Georgias's shop, and the moment after he saw his mum standing on the step of the house where he lived, looking anxiously up and down the street.

"Tom! Where have you been? I've been looking for you everywhere," she said as she hugged him.

So Tom explained that he had run away because he was so tired of everyone saying that how he looked and what he did were just like how the rest of the family looked and what the rest of the family did.

"But I found my way back from ever so far away by seeing the Number SEVEN bus with my own eyes. And I heard the canal boat's hooter with my own ears and I smelled Mr Georgias's delicious new bread with my own nose. So now I know that they are really mine and don't belong to anyone else. So I shan't have to run away again," said Tom.

Who's Afraid?

BERNARD ASHLEY

The big dog stood like a wolf, smack in Pleasure's way. It had come running out of nowhere and stopped in the middle of the path. Pleasure stopped, too. All right, she wasn't going far, just round the back of the flats to play, but she couldn't get there past this dog. It was an alsation, nearly as tall as she was, and its eyes were staring, none too friendly.

Pleasure stood a way back and waved her arms. "Shoo, boy!" she shouted.

But the dog only growled and scraped one of its front paws forwards, showed her a slice of white teeth and red gum—and Pleasure's next step was backwards.

The alsation barked. No warning. It suddenly barked, loud and very fierce.

Pleasure ran, scared—and cross with herself because she was scared—back into the flats to bang hard at her own front door. "I'm getting my daddy to you!" she shouted over her shoulder. "He ain't scared of dogs! He ain't scared of nothin'!"

Pleasure's daddy opened the door and stared down at the child. "What's all this commotion? Them boys after you again?"

"A big dog, barking at me!" Already, Pleasure was pulling at her daddy's arm.

"Yeah? I better have a talk with this here dog, then . . ."

Pulling him hard, Pleasure took her daddy round to where the big dog had been. And they hadn't got their shadows round the corner when 'Whoof!'—with a tremendous bark the alsation came top speed from behind the garages and stood to face them on the path.

"Whoa!" Mr Richard's voice had a warning in it. Without taking his eye off the dog, he scooped up Pleasure and held her in his arms.

"Get out the way! Shoo boy!" Pleasure suddenly felt safe enough to shout, trying to jump her daddy forwards. "Tell him!"

But what she got was a great big shake. "Hold your noise! That one's a stray." The man's voice was all quiet in his throat. "He's hungry. No one won't be tellin' him nothing!"

The dog started coming at them, one step then another, barking all the while. Pleasure's daddy started backing off, one step then another, getting faster all the while: till he turned and ran and slammed them in through the front door of the flats, dumping Pleasure down and holding the handle fast.

With a barking and scratching the dog threw itself at the door.

"I'm 'phonin' the police. That dog needs catchin'!"

The dog gave up and went sloping away. Pleasure looked up at her daddy. He was sweating. He'd been scared, too. That dog had made him run away—and him a daddy! She didn't know what to think about that. Did he get scared, too, then, sometimes? Was he just the same as her about some things?

She followed him indoors and poured herself a glass of Coke. Then, to cheer him up from his scare, too, she got out another glass and poured one out for her daddy.

Fuzzball

BERLIE DOHERTY

Fuzzball was the fattest bee in the garden. He loved to lollop into the deepest flowers hunting for pollen, and to buzz away with it to his hive. When he passed other bees he would smile his sticky smile and hum happily. He was the best bee, and he knew it. Sometimes he sat on the branches of the apple-tree and listened to the magpies chattering.

"Kwark! Kwark!" they'd go.

And "Buzz!" Fuzzball would say, as if he understood everything they were talking about.

One day he was fumbling about lazily, looking for brighter and deeper flowers to explore, and humming drowsily to himself, when he heard the sound of a huge bee singing. Fuzzball stopped for a minute and listened. He flew round the garden, knowing

48

that somewhere there was a fatter, louder bee than himself, and feeling very angry about it.

The singing came out of the house and into the garden, and Fuzzball bumbled about in amazement and alarm because he saw that it was coming from the fattest bee in the world, and that the fat bee was taking pollen from a huge yellow flower.

Fuzzball flew up to the apple-tree, but the magpies had scattered in fright. "Kwark! Kwark!"

The huge bee and the yellow flower sat down on a striped deckchair in the garden and kept on buzzing, and Fuzzball sat in the apple-tree and trembled. The huge bee was a man called Ben. He played in a band every Sunday. He'd come out in the garden in his black-and-gold bandsman's outfit to practise his saxophone and there he was, buzzing away happily, and not knowing how much fright he was giving to everyone.

But even though Fuzzball was frightened, he was greedy. He thought Ben's saxophone was the brightest flower he'd ever seen. The more he thought about it, the more he wanted to explore its dark mouth for the wonderful sweet pollen that must be inside it.

When Ben was quiet for a moment, Fuzz-ball took his chance. He flew to the rim of the saxophone and peered down it. It was deep and dark, like the heart of a golden lily. He hummed quietly to himself because he was very frightened, and plunged down.

That was when Ben started playing again. His saxophone rumbled like the buzzing of a whole hive of bees. Fuzzball tumbled about inside the noise. He couldn't climb out because the sides of the saxophone were so slippery. His head felt as if it would burst. He tossed about on the noisy wind of Ben's playing.

"Help!" he buzzed. "Help!"

At last Ben stopped playing. His tune wouldn't come right at all. He put his saxophone down in its red case and was just about to close the lid when he saw the little fat bee stumbling out of it.

"Blow me!" said Ben. "A bee! No wonder my tune wouldn't come right!"

And as for poor Fuzzball, he was so tired and he had such a headache that he had to walk all the way home to his hive.

And it was a long, long time before he came out of it again.

I'm a colour

NAOMI LEWIS

Here's a riddle poem. It's about a colour, and you must guess which it is.

I'm a colour; you guess what.
I am warm and I am hot.
I'm the one in fire and flame.
  Can you guess my name?

My cat Ginger is a clue,
Carrots and nasturtiums too;
Sunset, sunrise, marmalade,
You never see me in the shade.
Freckle-face has hair that colour;
Every other kind seems duller.
There's a fruit that has my name—
The fruit and colour are the same.
The answer? Well, it starts with O.
  I'm sure you know!

Two Trolls and a Trick

HELEN CRESSWELL

There are trolls living in the deep dark wood, big, bad trolls with big yellow teeth and dirty toes. But two of those trolls are not bad at all. Their names are Tig and Toggle, and no matter how hard they try to be bad, they always end up by doing someone a good turn.

One day a man went to the big bad trolls. "I've lost my cat in the wood," he said. "A big ginger pudding cat. If you can find him I'll give you a bag of gold as a reward."

Now the trolls in the deep dark wood are bad all right, but they're lazy as well. They wanted the gold, but they couldn't be bothered to look for the cat.

"*I* know what we'll do," said one of them. "We'll trick those two goody goodies Tig and Toggle into finding that cat for us."

So this is what they did. They went stamping up to the deep dark hole where Tig and Toggle lived.

"Listen!" they shouted. "We're going to be *really* bad today! There's a cat in the wood, a

big ginger pudding cat, and we're going to
catch it! Ho! Ho! Ho! *Ain't* we bad!"

And off they went.

"We can be just as bad as they are," said
Tig. "*We'll* catch the cat!"

"We'll take this net," said Toggle.

So off they went.

"Stamp stamp, we're going to be bad!
Stamp stamp, we're going to be bad!" they
yelled.

The other trolls heard them and grinned,
showing their big yellow teeth.

"Look!" said Tig. "There it is, up that
tree!"

And so it was, a big ginger pudding cat.

"I don't like the look of it," said Toggle. "It might bite!"

"I'll go up the tree," said Tig (he wasn't bad, but he was very brave indeed). "When the cat jumps—throw the net over him!"

Up he climbed and down jumped the cat and—wheeh! down came the net right over him.

"Hooray! Hooray!" yelled the two trolls. "Now off we go to find the big bad trolls. *We'll* show them how bad we can be!"

When they got back to their hole, the big bad trolls were there waiting. *Didn't* they grin when they saw that big ginger pudding cat in the net.

"We're bad now! We're bad at last!" shouted Tig.

"*Oh*, no you're not!" said the big bad trolls. "Here—*we'll* take the cat, and thank you very much for catching him for us. You've done your good deed for the day."

Off they went, and as they went they yelled, "We tricked you! Ho ho ho! We're off to get our reward for finding the cat! We're off to get our bag of gold. Ho ho ho!"

And so they did. And did they share that bag of gold with Tig and Toggle? They did not. They kept the whole bag for themselves.

Tig and Toggle stamped their feet and gnashed their teeth. "We'll pay you back!" they yelled. "We'll pay you back!"

But will they . . .?

Black and White

WILLIAM MAYNE

Harlequin mews at the window, a side dark, a side light.

"Who has come to visit me?" says Tabby. "A handsome gentleman, I think. How fine."

Her people say, "A black and white tomcat, with bitten nose and clawed-off ears, and bold, bad eyes, is looking in."

Tabby says to him, "Hello. My bowl of milk is better shared, there's enough for two."

Tomcat looks round, one eye black, the other white. He is not scared. "What a charming lady," he says. "So pretty and so bright." He takes a lick of milk.

"You say such clever things," says Tabby. "So kind."

He smiles. Moonlight is his favourite place, secret night his time. All night long the new-found friends sing on the roofs, jumping in the shadows of the moon. When the moon goes small, Harlequin's off.

"I'm a stay-at-home," says Tabby, quite content. "I'll always remember the words."

When the moon is large again Harlequin comes that way.

"Stay-at-home cat," says he, "will you come out to play?"

"I'm glad to see you, dear," says Tabby. "I fear I can't come out, I'm getting rather stout."

"It suits you dear," says Harlequin. "Ah well, there's another street I'll visit in. Good-night."

"Have fun," says Tabby. "I'll never forget the tune."

She goes from being stout, to being fat. And up and down the stairs she prowls. Her people find her lying in the bottoms of the beds; they find her looking in the wardrobes; they find her licking in the empty larder, or lurking in the attics.

The children one day see her tear up the daily paper. "Bad cat," they say. "See, Mother, what she's done."

"I know just how you feel, my Tabby cat," the mother says. She finds a strong new box, and puts in it the softest rags. Tabby looks in quite slow, feels with paws and claws, and says. "That's fine, that's mine; that's best for my nest."

"I'm a mother too," says the children's mother. "I know."

"Clever Tabby to have kittens," say the children.

"Poor silly things," says Tabby. "Would I have puppy dogs or rabbits? I'm so full of kittens, I'm a cushion, not a cat."

In the morning, she is lying in her nest slim and suprised, smoothing down her fur, and washing her three kittens, stopping only to mew and purr. She is so pleased.

The kittens are like her, and like Harlequin.

Kitten Trim is tabby like his mother, with white across his nose, most smilish; Kitten Tickin is white, and she has a black-tipped tail, most stylish; Kitten Tomkin is black with two white gloves and tabby waistcoat, quite Fair-Islish.

"What pets," the children say. "We'll keep them all."

"Of course," says Tabby. "I'll bring them up so well."

"We'll see, we'll see," says the mother of the house.

Harlequin comes sliding in to look. "Not bad," he says, "just like their dad. I suppose you'll be busy now."

"Indeed I am, my dear," says Tabby.

"I'll go," says Harlequin. "I am a vagabond cat, a stray."

"Goodbye, dear friend," says Tabby. "Have much fun. Farewell, farewell."

He kisses her upon the nose, goodbye, and off he goes, the wanderer; but where we cannot tell.

And They Began to Cry

WILLIAM MAYNE

The people of the house have all gone out. Tabby's three kittens, Tomkin and Tickin and Trim are all asleep.

She leaves them and goes out to stalk and stare and sit upon a wall, pounce and bounce, listen in the grass, think of mice and her wandering husband Harlequin.

She comes in and calls her kittens. There is no reply. The box that is their nest is empty when she looks in.

"What naughty things," she says, and listens. "But they are somewhere in the house."

She hears the one called Trim. He calls "Miau mama, miau," most pitiful and sad.

"Upstairs," says Tabby. "I'm coming, Trim. Stay still," and she twitches her tail. But when she's up he's down, and when she's down he seems up.

"Mama," he squeaks, "maMA," he shrieks. But where?

"Mama," squeals her middle one, Tickin. "Your Tomkin has been drowned all wetly wet."

Tabby leaves Trim. What squeaks can thrive, what's wet may not be alive. Tomkin's in the larder, drinking down a jug, until head first the milk drank him, sneezing in his nose, many bubbles in his ears. There's just his tail waving over the edge.

Tabby pulls the tail until the bubbles burst and out he comes. She licks his nose, slap slap; she's cross. "Go to the nest," she says.

She goes to look for Trim. He calls, "Mama MIAU mew mew," wild and scared.

Tickin's in the garden chasing butterflies. "I shan't eat you," she says. "It is a game."

Butterflies fly through the fence. They are not sure. Tickin follows them. She knows.

Man-next-door cuts his lawn today. He mows up a little kitten, and the butterflies fly away.

"My child," says poor Tabby. "She's chopped in two."

"Oh, no," says Man-next-door, "but I've shaved her tail quite hairless, and she's lost her whiskers, being careless."

"She is a sorry sight with her tail turned pink," says Tabby. "Go home to the nest. I still seek Trim.

Inside, and somewhere strange, is Trim. "I'm here," he says. "I don't know where. Don't you care, Mama mia miau?"

Where the mice live he has followed, where the pipes run, there he crawled, through a hidden hole he'd slid, between the kitchen and the hall, not in a room but in a wall.

There Tabby finds him, and she dusts him hard. "You're bad," she says. "Now I'm mad. Go to bed."

Off he goes, and there they all are, and Tabby with them.

"Oh, Mama," says Trim, with a little floorboard cough.

"Mew, mew," says Tickin, licking a tail with no black tip or fluff.

"Miau," says Tomkin, breathing out a bubbly, milky puff.

The people of the house come home. "Our quiet kittens and their mother," they say. "But one is milky, one is dusty, and the middle one's tail has turned quite pale. Did something happen, Tabby dear?"

"Nothing much," says Tabby. "A quiet day, quite typical. I knew they'd all be killed just once or twice. All the same, I'm glad it's at an end."

And she begins to purr.

Complaint of the cat called Whiskers

NAOMI LEWIS

I am a patient cat,
accepting this and that.
But I wish to make complaint,
and do not say I mayn't.
It's about my name.
I think it is a shame.
I want to change it now.
MAOUW! MIAOU! MIAOU!

Some cats have charming names
Like Jupiter or James,
Show Queen or Stripey,
Sheba or Benjamin.
But Whiskers, Sooty all us lot,
Do not like the names we've got.
We want to change them now.
MIAOW! MIAOW! MIAOW!

Gran's In-between Birthday

RACHEL ANDERSON

When Arthur's Gran came to stay, she brought Arthur a present.

"But it's not my birthday yet," said Arthur.

"I know dear," said his gran. "But I won't be here when it is."

Arthur was pleased with the book. It had pop-up pictures.

"Do you have birthdays?" Arthur asked Gran.

"Oh no dear. I'm much too old for all that now."

"How old?" Arthur asked. He thought it a shame that people got too old for birthdays.

"I can't remember," said Gran. "But I know I'm getting on."

"You were seventy-four last birthday," said Arthur's mum. "You ought to remember that!"

Arthur took the book with him to playgroup and, at storytime, he showed it to everybody. But Graham made a rude face and said,

"Arthur's stupid. It's not really his birthday."

Arthur didn't say anything back because he knew that people can have birthday surprises at any time of year. And anyway, he'd just had a good idea for his gran. At painting time, he asked for some white paper to make her a card.

"Ooh, lovely," said the playgroup helper. "Your gran's birthday, is it?"

"Not exactly," said Arthur.

On the card, Arthur painted a picture of a horse, which he knew his gran would like. When Gran fetched him from playgroup, she wanted to carry his things.

"No thank you," said Arthur, because he didn't want her to notice the card.

The next day, Wednesday, the middle day of the week, was always playgroup cooking day when everybody put on aprons. They were going to make currant scones. Arthur rolled his piece of mixture, and patted it, and squeezed it, and stuck the currants in it, and thought about his gran.

"Eeergh!" said Graham. "Arthur's scone looks horrible, like mud."

"No, it doesn't," said Arthur. "It's for my gran." And he took no notice of Graham and went on thinking about his gran.

The scones were cooked and, at milk-time, everybody ate theirs, except Arthur, who ran and put his in his coat pocket because he wanted to save it to take home.

When Gran came to fetch him she said, "Let me carry your coat, dear. It's nice and sunny today."

But Arthur kept his coat on because he didn't want Gran to know about his surprise till it was quite ready.

"Very well, dear," said Gran.

But at home, Arthur found that the scone had crumbled into bits inside his pocket. He showed his mum. She knew exactly what to do. First she helped him get the bits out, then she mixed some pink icing sugar in a bowl, then, while she was getting the dinner, Arthur iced the scone so that it was well stuck together. Mum found a cake candle to put on top too. After dinner, they closed the curtains, lit the candle and sang 'Happy Birthday dear Gran', and Arthur gave his gran the horse card.

Gran was surprised. "Well, I never!" she said. "I think an in-between birthday is the best kind of all."

When they ate the scone, it was a bit gluey inside, but the currants were all right, and so was the pink sugar. Afterwards, Gran had a little nap because people of seventy-four and a half get tired quite easily.

Tong and the Tomato

GERALDINE KAYE

Tong lives at the Hong Kong Take-Away with Father and Mother and Elder Sister and Second Sister and Small Sister.

One day, Elder Sister said, "What would you like for your birthday, Tong?" and she took him to the shop down the High Street to choose. Tong looked at the toys and sweets but he didn't want any of them, and then he saw the tomato plant.

"That's what I want," said Tong.

You're like Grandfather in Hong Kong," Elder Sister said. "Grandfather grows tomatoes and lettuces in boxes on his flat roof and he waters them every day."

But Tong couldn't remember Grandfather far away in Hong Kong.

Tong put his tomato plant on the window-sill at the back of the Hong Kong Take-Away and he watered it every day and the tomato plant grew and grew. Soon it was covered with creamy white flowers.

"With all those flowers you will soon have lots of tomatoes," Mother said.

But unfortunately the sparrows pecked off all the flowers.

"Sorry, sorry," Elder Sister said.

"Sorry, sorry," Second Sister said.

"Sorry, sorry," Small Sister said, but Tong was very sad.

Then Tong noticed there was just one creamy white flower left. So Tong went on watering his tomato plant every day just like Grandfather in Hong Kong—Tong thought he could remember Grandfather just a little bit now—and soon the one creamy white flower turned into a little green tomato. First, it was no bigger than a pea and then it was as big as a marble and then it was much bigger than that. The tomato grew and grew until it was very big indeed. And then it went yellow and orange and at last it was just as red as a tomato should be.

"It's the biggest tomato I have ever seen," Elder Sister said.

"It's the biggest tomato I have ever seen," Second Sister said.

"It's the biggest tomato there has ever been," Small Sister said.

Tong picked his tomato and cut it up. There was enough for Father and Mother and Elder Sister and Second Sister and Small Sister, Chai Eng, and for Tong, of course, and some for tomorrow as well as today.

But Tong kept one bit and dried it and took out the seeds. He kept three to grow on the windowsill next year and do you know what he did with the others? He put them in an envelope and sent them to Grandfather in far-away Hong Kong—to grow in the boxes on his flat roof.

Betty at the party

ANON

"When I was at the party,"
said Betty, aged just four.
"A little girl fell off her chair
And toppled on the floor.
All the other little girls
Began to laugh, but me—
I didn't laugh a single bit,"
said Betty seriously.

"Why not?" her mother asked her,
Full of delight to find
That Betty—bless her little heart—
Had been so poor and kind,
"Why didn't *you* laugh, Betty?
Or don't you like to tell?"
"I didn't laugh," the answer came,
"'cause it was me that fell."

Heave and Ho

KJARTAN POSKITT

This is the story of two tug boats, Heave and Ho. Their job was to guide big ships into harbour.

One day, Heave and Ho were resting quietly in the harbour, enjoying the sunshine.

"Can you see any ships coming?" asked Heave. "Any big ships that might need our help?"

"I can't see any," said Ho. "But I'll ask Egbert the crane. He's much taller than we are and he can see right over our heads. He can see for miles. Hey, Egbert!" she called. "Can you see any ships coming?"

Egbert stretched and stretched himself. He looked to the right and he saw plenty of clouds, plenty of sea and plenty of seagulls . . . but no big ships.

He looked to the left and he saw plenty of clouds . . . but no big ship. He saw the lighthouse though, and the lighthouse must have seen him because she winked at him . . . like this . . . just once.

Slowly, Egbert began to bend down when, quite suddenly, he saw something far away in the distance. He stopped and he looked and then he was sure. It was the biggest ship he had ever seen and it was coming straight towards them.

"Heave," called Egbert, "Ho, are you ready? Get ready to work. There's an enormous ship coming in."

And suddenly BOOM said the ship's horn, and everybody turned to watch it coming proudly towards the harbour.

Heave and Ho dashed quickly forwards.

"Hello," said Heave, breathlessly. "This is my sister, Ho, and we've come to guide you safely in."

"BOOM," said the big ship. "I don't need you. I can find my own way. Clear the path there, will you please?"

And it rumbled and snorted and gurgled its way past them.

"It's going too fast," said Heave.

"It's too near the pier," said Ho.

"We'd better follow," they said together.

All the people on the pier were watching and cheering the big ship as it came towards them.

Then suddenly an enormous wave crashed against its side, swung its nose round and in a second it was pointing right at the pier. Everyone began to run away.

"I can't stop," shouted the big ship.

"Up to us, now, Ho," said Heave, and as fast as he could he chugged right up behind the big ship. Quickly, he threw a rope onto its deck and then he pulled. With all his strength he pulled backwards. The water swirled and bubbled but still the big ship moved towards the pier.

Just then, Ho darted to the front of the ship. BANG. She butted her nose onto its side. She pushed and Heave pulled, and slowly, slowly the big ship turned away.

And how the people cheered.

"Well done, Heave," they shouted.

"Well done, Ho."

"I think", said Heave breathlessly, "we ought to take you to see Egbert the crane."

So the one big ship and the two little tugs sailed safely up to where Egbert was waiting for them.

"There could", said Egbert, standing very straight and tall, "have been a very nasty accident there. You two tugs are extremely brave."

"Boom," said the ship, but rather quietly. "I'm sorry I was so rude. Thank you for helping me."

And then, just to make sure everyone could hear him, he said it again, the loudest THANK YOU you could ever think of. The pier heard it and the harbour heard it, Egbert certainly heard it and so did all the people. Even the lighthouse heard it because she winked, just once.

"BOOM, BOOM!" said the big ship.

And the two little tugs were so pleased they went quite pink.

Things

MARJORIE DARKE

Pip liked collecting things. Anything. He stuffed his pockets with chalk and string, old keyrings, safety pins, pebbles and marbles, a whistle, a watch, broken laces, toffee papers, lots of lollipop sticks . . .

And GUM.

He loved chewing gum!

Everywhere he went he picked things up. Anything. Anywhere. Any time. Sundays, Mondays, Tuesdays . . .

On Wednesday morning he went to market with Dad. He found one empty cotton reel, two chewed pencils and three torn paper bags under a stall. He tucked all these into his pockets.

On Thursday afternoon Mum took him along when she went to dig the allotment. Pip dug too. He dug up four bits of broken pot, five bottle caps, and an old brass buckle. He didn't throw them away but crammed them into his bulgy pockets.

Not everything he found fitted his pockets. Some things were much too big. Punctured bikes and battered trikes, broken clocks, rusty padlocks, screwdrivers, kettles, buckets and cricket bats. Some he put in cardboard boxes and pushed them under his bed. Or shoved them into cupboards. Or piled them in the hall. The biggest things he leaned against walls in the kitchen, the bathroom, the garden shed—until doors wouldn't shut, windows wouldn't open and there was hardly room to move!

"You have too many things," Mum complained.

But Pip didn't listen. He went on collecting and collecting. By Friday he had even collected a dog!

The dog liked collecting things too . . . and eating them. Pip called him Hungry. Hungry dug up Mum's bulbs looking for bones. He chewed Dad's slippers, bit cushions and chased the cat. Leather, feathers and fur everywhere!

On Saturday, Dad shouted, "That dog will have to go!"

Pip left very quickly and took Hungry to visit Gran. On the bus he picked up six old tickets, one tiddlywink and a Have-A-Good-Day badge, and pushed them into his bursting pockets. Hungry found and ate an old shopping bag.

Gran's house was as neat as a pin. Everything in its place. Nothing to be found . . . except a big plate of sandwiches, a chocolate cake and a bowl of dog biscuits.

"Tuck in," said Gran. "After tea I have to collect things for a jumble sale. Would you like to help?"

"I'm good at finding things," Pip said.

So after tea they went all over Gran's house. They looked in cupboards and under beds. They hunted in the attic, the cellar, the garden shed. But there was almost nothing to find.

"Oh dear!" said Gran. "What shall I do?"

Pip thought. "I know. Have some of my things."

Gran took him home in her car. They went all over Pip's house looking in cupboards and under Pip's bed, *and* in the bathroom, the hall, the kitchen, the garden shed.

They found a mountain of things!

Old bikes and trikes. Padlocks and clocks. Keyrings, screwdrivers, kettles, buckets, cricket bats. A whistle, a watch, an old brass buckle, two jars full of marbles . . . and lots, lots more. So many things, Gran needed three trips in her car to collect them all.

Now doors shut again, windows could open and there was plenty of room to move.

But Pip did not give quite everything to Gran. One thing he kept, his favourite thing. Can you guess what it was?

A very Hungry dog!

Soup

DONALD BISSETT

Once, there was some soup. "I smell delicious!" said the soup. "I wonder what kind I am? Hm? Onion Soup. Tyrolese onion soup. Grandma's recipe, I think! Yum yum. I wish someone would taste me. Please, please come and taste me."

Just then a baby elephant came along. It was a big baby elephant. Baby elephants are!

The soup kept very quiet and tried hard not to smell delicious. It knew that if the elephant stretched out its trunk and went 'Schrllp!' all the soup would be gone in a moment. Though the soup wanted to be eaten, it didn't want to go in a big 'Schrllp!' but to be properly eaten, spoonful by spoonful, just like soup should be.

Then a mouse came along, "Sniff sniff!" went the mouse. It looked up at the plate of soup but it was too high to reach. The poor mouse started to cry, little tears ran down its nose." Then it heard a noise.

"Mieow!"

The mouse disappeared as fast as lightning.

"Mieow!" said the cat. "Soup!" It sniffed and turned away. "Cats don't like soup," it said.

The soup was indignant.

"Not like soup! Oh, wretched creature! Oh dear, I'm getting cold. I hope someone comes and eats me soon."

Two people did come, Twins. "Look," they said, when they saw the soup. "It smells delicious. Judi, you try it!" said Polly. "Let's both try it!" said Judi. "Look, there are two spoons."

The soup was very happy. "Goodbye, dear world!" it said. "I'm going to be eaten and that's what soup likes best.

Judi took a spoonful.

Polly took a spoonful.

"Mmm!" they said, "Yum yum, we do like soup!"

The soup was very happy. Just then Grandpa came along. "Good?" he said. "The soup is good?"

"Yes," said the Twins, "very good!"

"Oh dear!" said Grandpa. "I have just met a sad baby elephant. It wanted some soup, too.

82

But the soup was trying not to smell delicious. And it was such a small plate for an elephant, anyway!"

Grandpa glanced up and saw on the shelf a hundred packets of soup. He smiled. "Fifty should be enough!" he said. "We'll make the soup in the bathtub.

And they did, and then fetched Eli.

Eli sniffed with his trunk. He waggled his ears and swished his tail and looked down at the soup. Then, tenderly, making sure it was not too hot, he dipped his trunk into the soup and took a little 'Schrllp!' He took out his trunk and looked at the ceiling. "Oh yummity yummity!" he said and drank all the soup to the last drop . . . then slurped away.

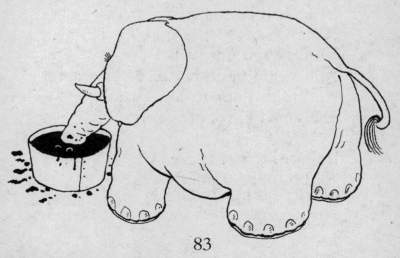

Jenny Wren

ANON

Jenny Wren fell sick
Upon a merry time.
In came Robin Redbreast
And brought her sops and wine.

"Eat well of the sops, Jenny,
Drink well of the wine."
"Thank you Robin, kindly.
You shall be mine."

Jenny Wren got well
And stood upon her feet.
And told, poor Robin, plainly
She loved him not a bit.

Robin, he was angry,
And hopped upon a twig,
Saying, "Out upon you, fie upon you,
Bold faced jig!"

The Girl and the Geese

ALAN GARNER

Once upon a time, an old man and his wife had a daughter and a son. And the mother said to the daughter, "Your father and I are off to market. While we are away, be very careful. Look after your little brother; and don't, whatever you do, go out of the house."

"Yes, mother," said the girl. But as soon as the old man and his wife were gone to market, she forgot what she had been told, and she left her brother sitting on the doorstep, while she went out to play hopscotch in the street.

And while she was playing hopscotch, a flock of wild geese came down out of the sky, and lifted the little boy onto their wings and flew away with him.

The girl saw the geese, and she ran after them, but they went into a dark wood.

The girl ran to the wood; and she saw a stove. And she said:

> "Stove, stove!
> Tell! Tell!
> Where have the geese gone?"

And the stove said, "Eat the burnt cake that is in my oven, and I'll tell you where the geese have gone."

> But the girl wouldn't;
> so the stove didn't;
> and the girl ran on.

She came to an apple tree; and she said:

> "Tree, tree!
> Tell! Tell!
> Where have the geese gone?"

And the tree said, "Eat the green apple that is on my branch, and I'll tell you where the geese have gone."

> But the girl wouldn't;
> so the tree didn't;
> and the girl ran on.

She came to a brook of milk with banks of pies; and she said:

"Brook, brook!
Tell! Tell!
Where have the geese gone?"

And the brook said, "Drink my sour milk and eat my sad pies, and I'll tell you where the geese have gone."

But the girl wouldn't;
so the brook didn't;
and the girl ran on.

She met a pig in the wood; and she said:

"Pig, pig!
Tell! Tell!
Where have the geese gone?"

"Into my sty," said the pig, "and thrown me out, they have! That's where the geese have gone!"

The girl ran till she came to the sty in the middle of the wood. And there was her little brother, sitting on the floor, and he was playing with apples of gold. She crept into the sty, picked him up in her arms, and ran out again.

But her little brother dropped the golden apples, and he began to cry; and the geese heard him and came flying to catch him again.

The girl ran to the brook of milk; and she said:

"Brook! Brook!
Hide me!
So the wild geese won't find me!"

And the brook said, "Drink my sour milk, and eat my sad pies."

And so the girl did;
and so the brook hid;
and the wild geese flew by.

The girl ran on, and soon she heard the geese coming after; and she ran to the apple tree, and she said:

"Tree! Tree!
Hide me!
So the wild geese won't find me!"

And the tree said, "Eat my green apple."

And so the girl did;
and so the tree hid;
and the wild geese flew by.

The girl ran on, and soon she heard the geese coming after her; and she ran to the stove, and she said:

"Stove! Stove!
Hide me!
So the wild geese won't find me!"

And the stove said, "Eat my burnt cake."

And so the girl did;
and so the stove hid;
and the wild geese flew by.

The girl ran on; she ran out of the wood, and all the way home. And a good job, too! For here come the old man and his wife, riding back from market!

The Froggy Princess

NICHOLAS FISK

A long time ago, when there were dragons and wicked witches and knights in armour and fairy tales were true, there lived a beautiful princess called Princess Amanda.

I said she was beautiful. Well, she was beautiful when she wasn't crying. But she was always crying. Her nose was always red from crying, and her eyes were puffy and pink from crying.

Why did she cry so much? Because she was waiting for a handsome Prince to come to the castle and marry her. But no Prince ever came. Not one.

One fine summer day, Princess Amanda cried harder than she had ever cried before. She wept *buckets*. She cried so much and for so long that the tall, narrow turret in which she lived began to fill with water. It was when the water had risen just above her knees that she saw the frog. The frog was swimming in the water with its back legs going Per-chung, Per-chung. Its bright round eyes stared straight at her.

"Go away!" said the Princess. "I hate frogs! All slippery and slimy! Ugh!"

The frog said, "Qu-arckk." Then, "Don't be rude."

"What did you say?" said Princess Amanda who was so surprised by the talking frog that she forgot to cry. "*What*?"

The frog hopped out of the water and into the Princess's lap.

It was then that the Princess noticed the frog was wearing a nice little gold crown. "Gracious me!" she said. "You're a Fairy-Tale Frog!"

"Quite right," said the frog in its croaky voice. "Really, I'm a handsome Prince. But a wicked witch cast a magic spell and turned me into a frog."

"Oh, how sad," said Princess Amanda, weeping more than ever.

"If a Princess kisses me," the frog said, "I'll turn back into a handsome Prince, with a sword at my side and a curly feather in my hat. You are a Princess, aren't you? Just one little kiss . . ."

"Kiss *you*?" said Princess Amanda. "Never!"

"We'll be married and live happily ever after," said the frog.

"Kiss a slimy, slippery *frog*?" said Princess Amanda. She sounded disgusted. But she was thinking he really is a very handsome frog, and he should turn out to be a very handsome Prince.

So she bent down, pulled a face and kissed the frog.

WHAM! BANG! WALLOP! BOOM!

There was thunder and lightning and drums and trumpets—and ABRACADABRA! The spell cast by the Wicked Witch was ended!

The trouble was that the spell ended the wrong way.

Instead of the frog turning into a Prince, the Princess turned into a frog. Yes, a girl frog, with a yellow tummy, green spots and stripes, and a little gold crown with pearls round the edge.

At first, Princess Amanda was furious. But soon she began to cheer up. She soon learned hopping, jumping and swimming—it was good fun. Being damp and watery did not bother her. She had spent all her life crying, so she was used to the wet. Best of all, her frog Prince was, to her eyes, very handsome indeed. And very popular. All the frogs cheered like anything when Princess Amanda became the Prince's bride. The underwater wedding was splendid.

Time passed and the couple had many royal children, some striped, some spotted and some a bit of both. So Princess Amanda gave up crying and, indeed, lived happily ever after.

Now, all this took place a long time ago. But even today, when you meet a frog—be careful. You should treat every frog with respectful politeness. Because, you see, your frog could be a royal frog; one of the great, great, great, great grandchildren of Princess Amanda.

Far away and long ago

NAOMI LEWIS

Far away and long ago—
That's where I want to go.
To ride up the glass mountain
To the kingdom of the snow,
To walk along the rainbow—
Where does it disappear?
The clouds look fine to walk on—
What am I doing here?
Oh, throw me up in a blanket
Till over the moon I'm swinging,
And if you listen down below,
Here's what I'll be singing.
How many miles to Babylon?
Three score and ten.
Shall I get there by candlelight?
Yes, there and back again!